This Little Tiger book belongs to:

_____

_____

_____

For Nicola, Eliza, Jack, and Tom
~ A. M.

For Miles, with love
~ J. M.

LITTLE TIGER PRESS
1 The Coda Centre,
189 Munster Road, London SW6 6AW
www.littletigerpress.com

First published in Great Britain 1995
by Little Tiger Press, London
This edition published 2012

Printed in China

2 4 6 8 10 9 7 5 3 1

Little Teddy Left Behind

Anne Mangan   Joanne Moss

LITTLE TIGER PRESS

Little Teddy woke up and sneezed loudly. Nobody
heard him because no one was there. Nicola and Jack
had moved to a new house.

"I'm all alone," said Teddy. "They've left me behind.
They never were very good at packing. I'm all dusty too,"
he said, and he sneezed and sneezed.

It grew dark, and at last Teddy went to sleep again . . .

. . . until the next morning when
the cleaning lady's dog spotted him
and picked him up.

"What have you got there?" asked
the lady, and when she saw how grubby
Teddy was, she grabbed him with her
big hands . . .

. . . and popped him into the washing machine!

"Oh, help!" cried Little Teddy, but nobody heard his tiny squeak.

It was awful in the washing machine. Teddy was whirled around and around until he was dizzy. He growled his very loudest growl, but nobody came to rescue him.

At last, he was spun dry and the machine stopped. Teddy lay there among all the damp clothes, wondering what would happen next.

The cleaning lady opened the machine door and took out Teddy. "You're not quite dry yet," she said.

"Yes, I am!" growled Little Teddy, but she took no notice and pinned him upside-down on a clothesline.

"I'd rather be dirty and the right way up!" he cried, but of course nobody heard his tiny squeak.

It was windy, and
Teddy swung back
and forth on the clothesline.
It was exciting in a way, like flying in space.
All at once the line broke, and Teddy fell down, down, down into the grass. Butterflies flew all around him and bees buzzed over his head. Teddy liked the bright cheerful butterflies, but he was a bit afraid of the bees.

"You scare me," he squeaked, but the bees were too busy to hear him.

Suddenly Teddy felt hot breath in his ear.

"Oh, no!" he cried. "It's that dog again!"
	The dog seized the little bear in his big teeth
and pushed through a very prickly hedge into
the next yard.
	"Oh, my poor fur!" gasped Teddy.
	A lady looked up as the dog rushed onto her lawn.
"Ugh, he's got a rat in his mouth!" she screamed
and threw a gardening glove at them.
	"I'm not a rat!" growled Teddy.

The dog ran out through
the gate into the woods.

"Oh, I wish he'd drop me," thought Teddy, and at
last he did. The dog spotted a rabbit and ran off, leaving
Teddy behind.

Teddy lay very still, hoping the dog wouldn't come back.
It was quiet in the woods—but not for long. Two children
came rushing toward him.

"Hey, a little teddy bear!" cried one of the children.

"That's me," thought Teddy. "Now what?"

He soon found out.

"Catch!" the boy yelled, and poor Teddy
was tossed from one to the other until he felt a bit
sick. Jack and Nicola had never played with him like this.

At last the children grew tired of their game, and the
girl flung Little Teddy high into the air.

Up, up, up he sailed, right into the branches of a tall
tree. No sooner had he landed than he heard an angry
chittering noise.

"Trying to steal my nuts, are you?"

Teddy looked down. At the end of his branch, a squirrel was glaring at him. Teddy tried to explain about the boy and girl and their awful game of catch, but the squirrel didn't seem to hear. "This is my tree!" he said, giving Teddy a sudden push.

The little bear fell down, down, down . . .

. . . and landed on a wooden floor.

He was lying there, getting his
breath back and worrying whether Jack
and Nicola would ever find him again,
when he heard children's voices. He tried
his growl and he tried his squeak, but
they were too small for the children to
hear him.

The floor was as dusty as the empty
room he had left behind. Once again
Little Teddy began to sneeze and sneeze.
The sneezes were louder than the growl
and the squeak, and at last the voices
came nearer . . .

"Look, there's a ladder!"

"It's a tree house!"

Two faces were peering at him—two faces he knew very well!

"It's Little Teddy!" cried Jack. "How did he get into our new back yard? I thought he was all packed up."

"I don't know, but it doesn't matter," said Nicola, giving Teddy a hug. "We've found Teddy *and* a tree house."

"It's Teddy's tree house," said Jack. "He found it."

His very own house! Little Teddy liked the idea.

A few days later, Nicola and Jack had a
housewarming party for all their friends.
Each friend brought a teddy bear, so that Little
Teddy could have his own friends at his own
housewarming in his new home in the big tree.